For Jenny and Michael,
with love from
J.A.

For David, Brigitte, Chlöe, Christof and Dimitri
T.H.

The author and publisher wish to thank
Martin Jenkins for his invaluable
assistance in the preparation of this book.

First published 1993 by Walker Books Ltd
87 Vauxhall Walk, London SE11 5HJ

This edition published 1999

2 4 6 8 10 9 7 5 3 1

Text © 1993 Judy Allen
Illustrations © 1993 Tudor Humphries

This book has been typeset in Times New Roman.

Printed in Hong Kong

British Library Cataloguing in Publication Data
A catalogue record for this book is available from the British Library.

ISBN 0-7445-6354-2

SEAL

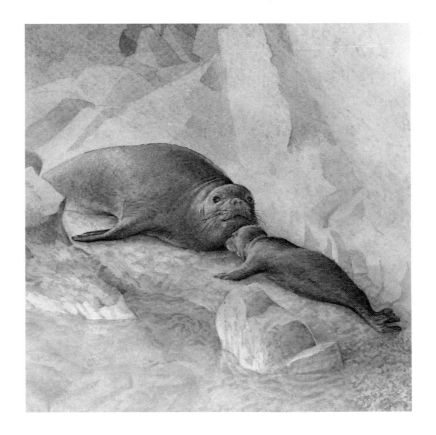

Written by
Judy Allen

Illustrated by
Tudor Humphries

WALKER BOOKS
AND SUBSIDIARIES
LONDON · BOSTON · SYDNEY

"One day," said Jenny, "I want to know something that none of you know." She was on holiday in Greece with her mother, her father and her big brother Joe. Every day, for nearly two weeks, the three of them had told her things. They had told her stories about the ancient Greek gods. They had explained how the ruined temples and broken statues had once looked. They had shown her little white churches, huge hillside monasteries, and trees growing olives and lemons. They had taught her how to eat an artichoke; and how to recognize a swallowtail butterfly, a spider crab, a stinging jellyfish.

Now, sitting outside a café, eating honey cakes, Jenny decided her head was so full it didn't have room for a single extra piece of information.

Her father pointed across the small harbour to an island that rose from the sea like a miniature mountain.

"We must get a caique to take us out there," he said. "Jenny, a caique is a kind of boat."

Jenny put her hands over her ears. "Don't tell me anything more!" she said.

"You mustn't mind us knowing more than you," said her mother. "We're all older than you are."

"But you'll always be older than me," said Jenny. "I'll never catch up."

Later, down by the boats that were moored in the shallows, Jenny's father talked with two fishermen. The older one spoke only Greek. His son Stefanos, though, could speak English.

Stefanos was friendly, but he shook his head when Jenny's father asked about a trip to the island.

"It is only a rock," he said. "No one goes there."

"We'd like to have a picnic on it," said Jenny's mother.

"Not possible," said Stefanos. "There are many other rocks under the sea around it. The bottom

would be torn out of my boat. Instead
I will take you night-fishing, if you
would like?"

"We would like!" said Joe.

"Then we go tonight," said
Stefanos cheerfully.

The evening sun was still making a glowing red path across the sea when they got into the boat, but Stefanos lit the lamps at once. They hissed softly as they burned.

"They're gas lamps," said Joe. "That's why they make that sound."

Jenny ignored him.

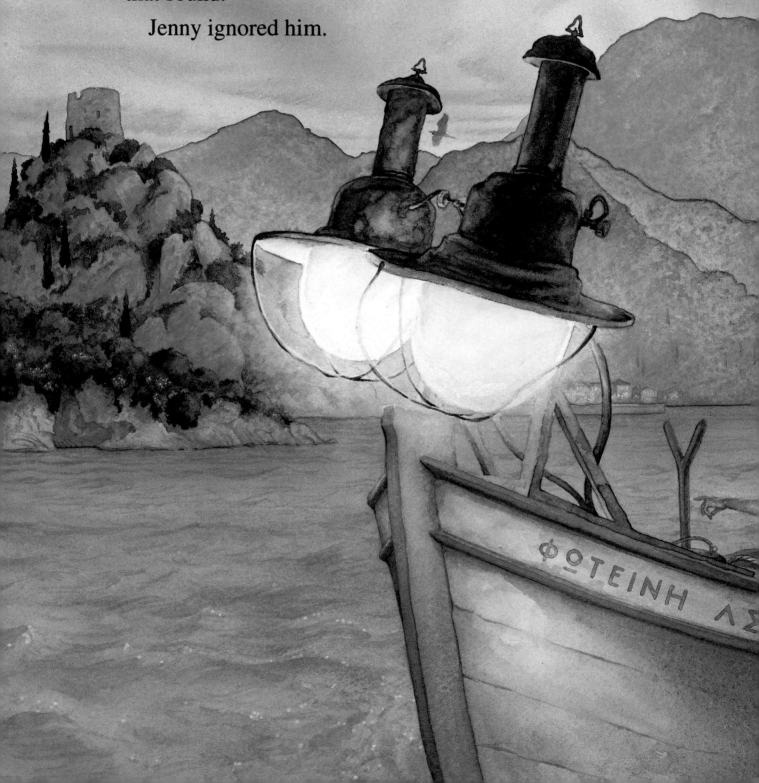

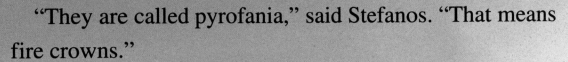

"They are called pyrofania," said Stefanos. "That means fire crowns."

Jenny smiled. She liked the name – and she found she didn't mind Stefanos telling her things.

His boat had an engine, but he didn't use it. He rowed out onto the darkening sea.

Jenny's mother pointed back towards the land, where a thousand tiny glimmerings flickered among the shadowy trees.

"Fireflies!" she said.

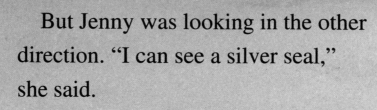

But Jenny was looking in the other
direction. "I can see a silver seal,"
she said.

"Are there seals in Greece?" said
Jenny's father.

"Not silver ones!" said her mother.

"Where is it?" said Joe.

"It's gone now," said Jenny.

Stefanos said nothing. He stopped
rowing and lowered a net into the
water. "We may get fish here,"
he said. "They come to the light."

"There!" said Jenny, half standing up and making the boat rock. "There it is!"

Something pearly white was moving towards them, trailing shimmering streaks through the water.

"Jenny's right, it *is* a seal," said Joe.

"It isn't really silver," said his father, as the seal submerged. "There's phosphorescence in the water." He began to explain about the microscopic sea creatures that glow nearly as brightly as fireflies, but Jenny wasn't listening. "Where's it gone?" she said.

"They are rare and shy," said Stefanos. "I think it will go far away."

"Well spotted, Jen," said Joe.

Jenny hardly saw the little shoal of whitebait they caught that night, or the small octopus. She stared at the sea until Stefanos rowed them back to the harbour – but the silver seal did not appear again.

When she saw it next day it no longer looked silver –
it was brown and glossy. She stood at the edge of the sea,
near Stefanos and his father, who were sorting their nets,
and watched it through her mother's binoculars.

Joe tried to interest her in a row of octopuses hanging
out to dry in the sun, but Jenny took no notice of him
and he wandered off.

"They all tell me things," she complained to Stefanos.

"I give you something to tell them," said Stefanos. "Your
seal is a monk seal."

His father spoke crossly. Stefanos shook his head and pointed to a boat on the horizon. "He says the seals take our fish," he explained to Jenny. "I tell him it is the big fishing boats that do that."

The old man grumbled again. "He says the seals get caught in the nets and tear them," said Stefanos. "That is true, but it doesn't happen often."

"Do the seals get out of the nets again?" said Jenny.

"Sometimes," said Stefanos. "But sometimes they drown."

Later, Jenny got a fright and called out to Stefanos. "My seal dived," she said, "and he hasn't come up again. He must be caught in a net."

"They stay underwater for a long time," said Stefanos.

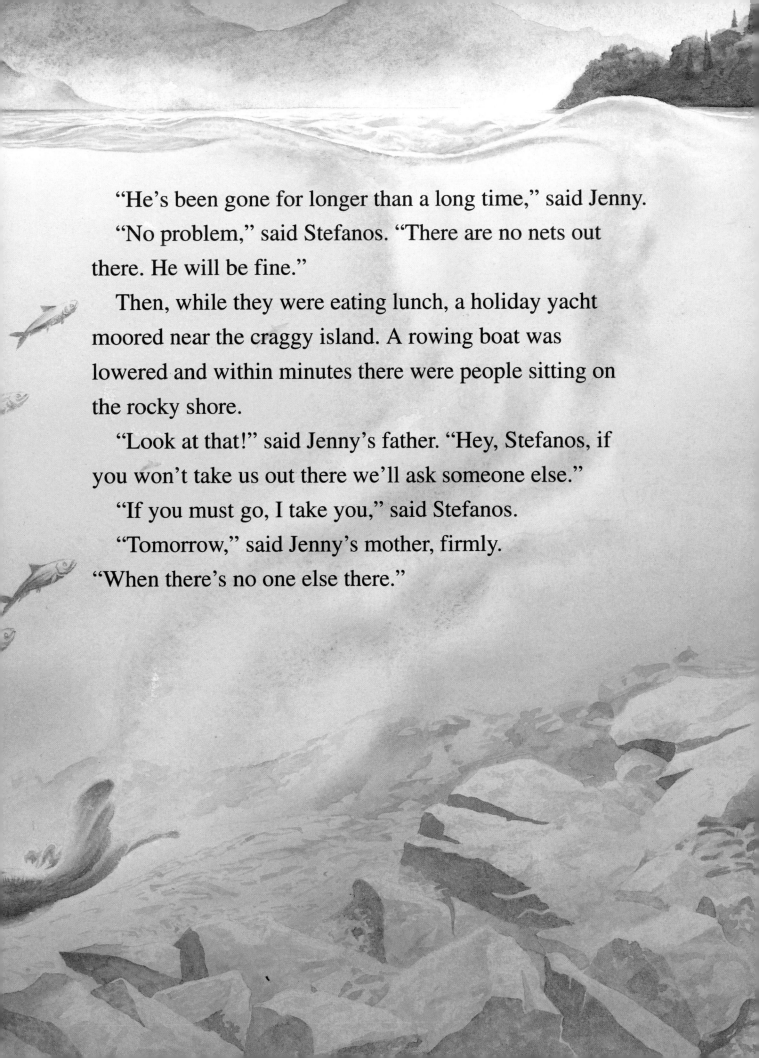

"He's been gone for longer than a long time," said Jenny.

"No problem," said Stefanos. "There are no nets out there. He will be fine."

Then, while they were eating lunch, a holiday yacht moored near the craggy island. A rowing boat was lowered and within minutes there were people sitting on the rocky shore.

"Look at that!" said Jenny's father. "Hey, Stefanos, if you won't take us out there we'll ask someone else."

"If you must go, I take you," said Stefanos.

"Tomorrow," said Jenny's mother, firmly. "When there's no one else there."

They went in the morning, with a bag of food and a
bundle of beach towels. The tiny island was further
away than they had realized, and this time Stefanos
used the engine. When they drew near, though, he shut it off.

"I cannot go closer," he said.

Looking down through the clear water, Jenny saw
tiny fish swimming among the dark rocks that grew
out of the sandy sea bed.

Her father jumped out first. The water reached
nearly to his waist. "Come on, Jen," he said,
"I'll give you a piggyback."

Joe balanced the picnic bag on his head and his mother
held the towels high. Stefanos watched them wade ashore.
"I will be nearby, fishing," he called. "Any time you say,
I will take you to a beautiful beach."

"He really doesn't like people coming here, does he?"
said Jenny's father quietly. "I can't imagine why."

He found a flat rock to lie on while his shorts dried.
Jenny's mother found a pool full of sea anemones.
Joe found two caves. The sun shone through a hole
in the roof of one, but the other was shady enough to
keep the picnic cool.

Stefanos rowed a little way off and lowered baskets to
catch squid.

Jenny clambered to the top of the rock-island to watch
for her seal. After a little while, Joe passed her lunch up
to her – bread, crumbly goat's cheese, an enormous tomato,
and some cherries.

Suddenly the seal appeared from nowhere, making her
jump. It looked straight at her, then dived. This time
Jenny had a good view, but though she stared for so long
that she dribbled tomato pips down her front,
it did not come up again.

There must be a cave under the island, Jenny thought.
She left the remains of her lunch, and crossed the top
of the island to the slope on the other side.

She could see Stefanos, in his boat, but she couldn't tell if he was watching her. Her family were too busy eating to look up. She lay on her stomach and stared down – and a sleek head popped out of the water below her. For a moment she was only a couple of feet from the sad, whiskery face, then the seal somersaulted and sent up a flurry of sand. When the sand settled, the seal was gone.

You definitely have a cave, thought Jenny, but I'm not following you underwater to find it. Then she remembered Joe's first cave, with the hole in the roof. Perhaps this one is the same, she thought.

It didn't take her long to find the jagged opening, half hidden by a little scrubby bush. She knelt down and peered through it.

At first all she could see was a
pattern of shimmering green and gold. Then she
could make out a huge dim cavern, with a stony floor
and shelves of rock. The sun shone through the shallow
sea and in at the underwater opening, lighting everything
with a watery glow.

There was a movement at the edge of the water, and the
seal appeared, hauling himself out of the water and on to the
little shingly cave-beach. Higher up, where the sea did not
reach, three more seals were resting – and two of them had
babies, lying close. Jenny could hear the sighing of the sea
and the soft bleating of one of the seal pups.

For what seemed like a hundred years she crouched
there, enchanted. Then she realized that, at last,
she knew something that not one of the rest
of her family knew.

She stood up – and saw that Stefanos was bringing his
boat closer, shouting and waving. "There is a squall
coming," he called. "You must come – I have to get my
boat in to harbour."

In the rush, Jenny had no time to say anything,
especially as Joe carried her out first, then waded back to
help the others collect their belongings.

Stefanos kept the boat steady and spoke to her softly.
"I know what you found," he said. "Their last hiding
place. I must tell you that if they are disturbed the
mothers may abandon the babies, or even kill them."

"I didn't disturb them," said Jenny, horrified.

"No," said Stefanos, "but will you betray them?"

"My family wouldn't hurt them!" said Jenny.

"Wouldn't they want to look?" said Stefanos. "Wouldn't
they dive down, just once? And wouldn't others hear of it,
and come out to see?"

"But I *really* want to tell them," said Jenny, as the family waded towards them.

"I understand," said Stefanos. "I give you something else to tell, instead." He thought for a moment. Then, "Hundreds of years ago," he said, "people believed that a tent made of sealskin would protect them from lightning."

Jenny frowned.

"And," said Stefanos, "they believed that if they dragged the skin of a seal round a field the crops would not be damaged by hailstones."

Jenny looked back at her family, wading out towards the boat.

"Will you keep the secret?" said Stefanos. "For the seals?" Then he turned to help the others on board.

The water became choppier and the rain began to fall as they travelled back. Jenny sat very quiet, very still.

"Someone doesn't mind the bad weather," said Jenny's father, as the seal's head broke the surface behind the boat.

"It's always alone, isn't it?" said her mother.

"I can tell you something none of you know," said Jenny.

"What?" said Joe.

Jenny told the story about the sealskin and the lightning.

"What an extraordinary thing," said her mother.

"How did you find that out?" said her father.

Jenny looked at them. They were all listening to her with interest. She couldn't remember that they had ever done that before. "I can tell you something else, too," she said.

Stefanos watched her. The seal sank below the surface, leaving a ring of water.

Jenny drew a deep breath. Then she told the story about the sealskin and the hailstones. "That's all," she said.

Stefanos smiled broadly. "Believe me," he said, "Jenny is wiser than you know."

SEAL FACT SHEET

THE MEDITERRANEAN MONK SEAL is the rarest seal in the world. In ancient times, many thousands of them used to live in the Mediterranean and off the North African coast of the Atlantic Ocean. Today there are almost certainly no more than 700 — and probably fewer than 500 — altogether, and the number gets smaller every year. Most of the seals live around the Greek islands of the Aegean, but there are still some in the Atlantic.

As well as the Mediterranean monk seal, another species, the Hawaiian monk seal, still survives in the Pacific Ocean. Sadly, a third species, the Caribbean monk seal, became extinct about thirty years ago.

◆ WHAT ARE THE DANGERS FOR SEALS? ◆

Fishermen have persecuted monk seals for hundreds of years, because they are thought to damage fishing nets and eat too many fish. The seals have been shot, they have been left to drown in fishing nets, and the caves where they have their young have been dynamited. Tourist developments have also destroyed many good breeding sites, and tourist boats often bother the mothers and young. The seals are very sensitive, and the mother finds it very difficult to raise her pups when disturbed in this way.

◆ IS ANYONE HELPING SEALS? ◆

Yes. Concerned scientists and organizations like WWF (World Wide Fund for Nature) have tried to find ways to stop fishermen from killing monk seals, and attempted to persuade governments to set up sanctuaries for them.

◆ ARE EFFORTS TO SAVE SEALS SUCCEEDING? ◆

Unfortunately, not very well. The population seems to be getting smaller every year. Even where the seals are not persecuted by people they may suffer from natural accidents and disease. For instance, off the coast of Mauritania in North Africa in the 1980s, many seals were killed when a cave fell in on top of them. Since then, nearly half the population there has died of disease.

◆ IS THERE ANYTHING YOU CAN DO? ◆

Yes. You can join the junior section of WWF or Greenpeace, or persuade your family or your school to join.

WWF	Greenpeace
Panda House	Canonbury Villas
Weyside Park	London
Godalming GU7 1XR	N1 2PN
United Kingdom	United Kingdom

MORE WALKER PAPERBACKS
For You to Enjoy

ANIMALS AT RISK
by Judy Allen/Tudor Humphries

Judy Allen has twice been shortlisted for the
BP Conservation Award. Her book, *Awaiting Developments*,
won the Friends of the Earth Earthworm Award and the
Whitbread Children's Novel Award and was Commended for the
Carnegie Medal. Among her many other books with an ecological
theme is the acclaimed *Anthology for the Earth*.

Each of these fine books in the Animals at Risk series
absorbs and informs. The series alerts readers to the dangers
facing some of the world's best-loved animals through
thoughtful and exciting child-centred stories.
How many have you got?

EAGLE	ELEPHANT	PANDA
0-7445-6351-8	0-7445-6352-6	0-7445-6353-4

SEAL	TIGER	WHALE
0-7445-6354-2	0-7445-6355-0	0-7445-6356-9

£4.99 each

Walker Paperbacks are available from most booksellers, or by post from
B.B.C.S., P.O. Box 941, Hull, North Humberside HU1 3YQ
24 hour telephone credit card line 01482 224626

To order, send: Title, author, ISBN number and price for each book ordered, your full name and address,
cheque or postal order payable to BBCS for the total amount and allow the following for postage and packing:
UK and BFPO: £1.00 for the first book, and 50p for each additional book to a maximum of £3.50.
Overseas and Eire: £2.00 for the first book, £1.00 for the second and 50p for each additional book.

Prices and availability are subject to change without notice.